EARLY BIRD
STORIES

Too Much Noise!

Early ★ Reader

First American edition published in 2021 by Lerner Publishing Group, Inc.

An original concept by Cath Joness
Copyright © 2022 Cath Jones

Illustrated by Leesh Li

First published by Maverick Arts Publishing Limited

Maverick
arts publishing

Licensed Edition
Too Much Noise!

Lerner Publications Company
An imprint of Lerner Publishing Group, Inc.
241 First Avenue North
Minneapolis, MN 55401 USA

For reading levels and more information, look up this title at www.lernerbooks.com.

Main body text set in Mikado. Typeface provided by HVD Fonts.

Library of Congress Cataloging-in-Publication Data

Names: Jones, Cath, 1965– author. | Li, Leesh, illustrator.
Title: Too much noise! / Cath Jones ; illustrated by Leesh Li.
Description: First American edition. | Minneapolis : Lerner Publications, 2021. | Series: Early bird readers. Yellow (Early bird stories) | "First published by Maverick Arts Publishing Limited"—Page facing title page. | Audience: Ages 4–8. | Audience: Grades K–1. | Summary: "Young children can practice their reading skills with this story about a bear with a loud, rumbly tummy and the rabbit friend who finds food to help fill his hungry belly"— Provided by publisher.
Identifiers: LCCN 2021001329 (print) | LCCN 2021001330 (ebook) | ISBN 9781728436852 (library binding) | ISBN 9781728438726 (paperback) | ISBN 9781728437811 (ebook)
Subjects: LCSH: Readers (Primary)
Classification: LCC PE1119.2 .J665 2021 (print) | LCC PE1119.2 (ebook) | DDC 428.6/2—dc23

LC record available at https://lccn.loc.gov/2021001329
LC ebook record available at https://lccn.loc.gov/2021001330

Manufactured in the United States of America
1-49646-49574-4/13/2021

EARLY BIRD STORIES

Too Much Noise!

Cath Jones

Illustrated by **Leesh Li**

Lerner Publications ◆ Minneapolis

Deep in the dark woods, Bear was in bed.

Deep in the dark woods, Rabbit was in bed.

But Rabbit's bed shook!

Rabbit got up.

Rabbit ran to Bear, deep in the woods.

"Bear!" said Rabbit.

"Too much noise. It's your tummy!"

"I need food," said Bear
with a big moan.

"I will get you food," said Rabbit.

He got nuts for Bear.

Crunch, crunch.

But Bear was not full.

So, Rabbit got Bear
some berries.

Burp!

But Bear was still not full!

Rabbit got Bear a big fish.

"Yum! Yum!
I am full!" said Bear.

"I need to go to sleep, Bear," said Rabbit.

Rabbit was snoring!

"Rabbit!" said Bear.

"Too much noise!"

Quiz

1. Where do Rabbit and Bear live?

   a) Deep in the woods

   b) At the beach

   c) In a big house

2. What does Bear need?

   a) A hug

   b) Water

   c) Food

3. What did Rabbit get Bear first?

   a) Nuts

   b) Seeds

   c) Fish

4. "Yum! Yum! I am _____!"
   said Bear.
   a) Loud
   b) Full
   c) Thirsty

5. What does Rabbit do at the end?
   a) Go home
   b) Eat all the food
   c) Make too much noise

COLOR		GRL
Silver	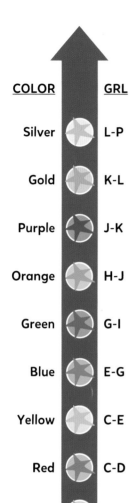	L-P
Gold		K-L
Purple		J-K
Orange		H-J
Green		G-I
Blue		E-G
Yellow		C-E
Red		C-D
Pink		A-C

EARLY BIRD STORIES

Leveled for Guided Reading

Early Bird Stories have been edited and leveled by leading educational consultants to correspond with guided reading levels. The levels are assigned by taking into account the content, language style, layout, and phonics used in each book.